Imani and Her Red Dancing Shoes

O.L. Harrison

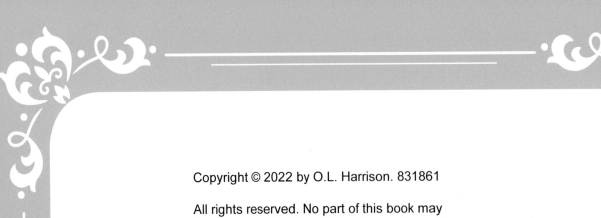

To order additional copies of this book, contact:
Xlibris
844-714-8691
www.Xlibris.com
Orders@Xlibris.com

ISBN: Softcover   978-1-6698-0056-9
        EBook   978-1-6698-0055-2

Print information available on the last page

Rev. date: 04/14/2022

Imani and Her
Red Dancing Shoes

Hi, my name is Imani, and my name means Faith. Since I was three years old, I have loved music and dancing. When I dance, my family would always clap and say nice things. When I was about ten years old, I started to imagine myself before millions of people performing. The people would be so happy, clapping and smiling as I performed.

After school, my parents would take my brother Sharod Jr. and me to the park.

Oh, my brother was named after our father. My brother loved playing football and rock climbing with his friends. I loved the park because so many people would always be there; when I dance, the people would circle around and watch. People would be smiling and clapping. They even gave me money at the end.

4

The trees would dance with me as the wind blew, the birds sang sweet melodies, the squirrels cracked nuts to the beat, the ducks quacked, and the frogs would whistle. Even the dogs barked and the cats patted their feet.

6

While in the park one day, a shiny star appeared to me. She had a long purple robe lined with gold trim and gold saddles, and she had beautiful light-brown skin and gorgeous light-brown eyes. She stretched out her hand to me, and I touched her hand.

Suddenly, we appeared in Italy at the Accademia Nazionale di Santa Cecilia in Rome. The orchestra was performing, and dancers were dancing. Wow, the orchestra was amazing, and the dancers danced with so much grace and poise.

As I sat in the balcony, joy filled my heart. I didn't even think to ask why was I there. I saw myself performing. I shook my head, but it was me! Then she brought me back to the park, and she was gone. Time just seemed as it stopped until I arrived back. I ran to tell my parents.

My father said, "Imani, wow, God sent you an Angel!"

I was smiling from ear to ear. As I was leaving at the end of the park entrance, I saw a beautiful pair of red dancing shoes. I heard God say to me, "Imani, this is one of your gifts you are created to be."

My mom smiled at me and said, "Those must be for you from the Lord."

I sat at the entrance and put on those red shoes. My mom said, "Come on, Imani, it looks like rain!" Wow! I danced with so much joy all the way home.

The next day, my parents encouraged me to try out for the dance team at school. When I arrived at school, I signed up for the dance team. The tryout was at the end of the day, so I could hardly wait! At the tryout, there were three judges and Ms. Christian. She stated the way I dance was ministry, and I was accepted. Later, Ms. Christian introduced me to a teacher who taught advance dance; her name was Ms. Joy. Each day, I could not wait for practice. Ms. Joy prayed at each practice and read the Bible too. She helped bring out the gift of dancing within me. Ms. Joy always said dancing was a gift.

One day, Ms. Joy said to me that she had signed me up for a recital at a local school. After the recital, I received great reviews. Ms. Joy later received a letter from the governor's office requesting for me. We were all excited, but Ms. Joy told me that God had blessed me, so I would have to come up with the routine on my own. I prayed to God for His blessings to rest upon me.

The day of the performance, I grabbed my red dancing shoes and off I went. I truly felt the presence of the Lord with me. Many doors opened up for me. I have performed in Greece, Australia, China, Canada, Italy, Roman, Paris, New York, and even Africa, just to name a few! I have always performed with a pair of red dancing shoes.

I have opened up a studio named Imani and Her Red Dancing Shoes, where we have teachers that share their gift of dancing to children in our community. We will be taking a group of exceptional dancers to Italy this summer, sharing the gift of God has given them! I encourage each of you to share the gift that God has given you for all the world to see! For with God, all things are possible (Matthew 19:26). God believes in *you!*

I am Imani.

Printed in the United States
by Baker & Taylor Publisher Services